W9-ANT-852

My Mommy
Hung the Moon

A Love Story

Jamie Lee Curtis & Laura Cornell

JOANNA COTLER BOOKS
An Imprint of HarperCollinsPublishers

Thanks to all my mothers; my friends, who have taught
me so much about being a wife and mother, and to Chris
and Annie and Tom for making me one; to Joanna, Laura,
Heidi, Phyllis, Kelly, and the team at HC, my gratitude is
as bright as the moon in this beautiful book.
—J.L.C.

To all at HarperCollins who, time after time, help me
and save me in this process of creation. You are many.
Thank you. To Jamie, always, for the wonderful words
and big thoughts; to Joanna, for her vision and cheers;
and to Carla, for bringing it all to life.
—L.C.

Books to Grow By is a trademark of Jamie Lee Curtis.
My Mommy Hung the Moon: A Love Story

Text copyright © 2010 by Jamie Lee Curtis Illustrations copyright © 2010 by Laura Cornell
All rights reserved. Printed in the United States of America. No part of this book may be used or
reproduced in any manner whatsoever without written permission except in the case of brief quotations
embodied in critical articles and reviews. For information address HarperCollins Children's Books,
a division of HarperCollins Publishers, 10 East 53rd Street, New York, NY 10022.
www.harpercollinschildrens.com

Library of Congress Cataloging-in-Publication Data
Curtis, Jamie Lee.
My mommy hung the moon : a love story / Jamie Lee Curtis ; Laura Cornell. — 1st ed.
p. cm. Summary: A hard-working mother's extraordinary accomplishments are listed by her devoted child.
ISBN 978-0-06-029016-0 (trade bdg.) ISBN 978-0-06-029017-7 (lib. bdg.) [1. Stories in rhyme.
2. Mothers—Fiction.] I. Cornell, Laura, ill. II. Title. PZ8.3.C9344My 2010   2009025450   [E]—dc22

10 11 12 13 14 LPR 10 9 8 7 6 5 4 3 2 1   ❖   First Edition

For Mom and Dad,
who hung the moon
in different and wonderful ways
—L.C.

For my mother, Janet Leigh
—J.L.C.

My mommy hung the moon.
She tied it with string.
My mommy's good at
everything.

She lit up the sun,
so bright and so round.
She puffed out each cloud,
stretched trees from the ground.

When she pours down rain so it's wet and dark,
I climb up on her like she's Noah's ark.

She zaps out the thunder and makes lightning glow,
then crayons for me a giant rainbow.

She feathered the birds. She taught them to chirp.

—burp

—burp

She taught me to speak, my cousin to burp.

She grows all the food

and makes it from scratch . . . .

. . . and when she bakes me cookies,

DOUGH LOG
makes 2 dozen

She writes all the books.

She made me TV.
She drew every 'toon, boxed all DVDs.

She webbed all the world, she dotted .com.
She e'd the email, my own CD MOM.

My mommy's the boss. She drives in the pool.

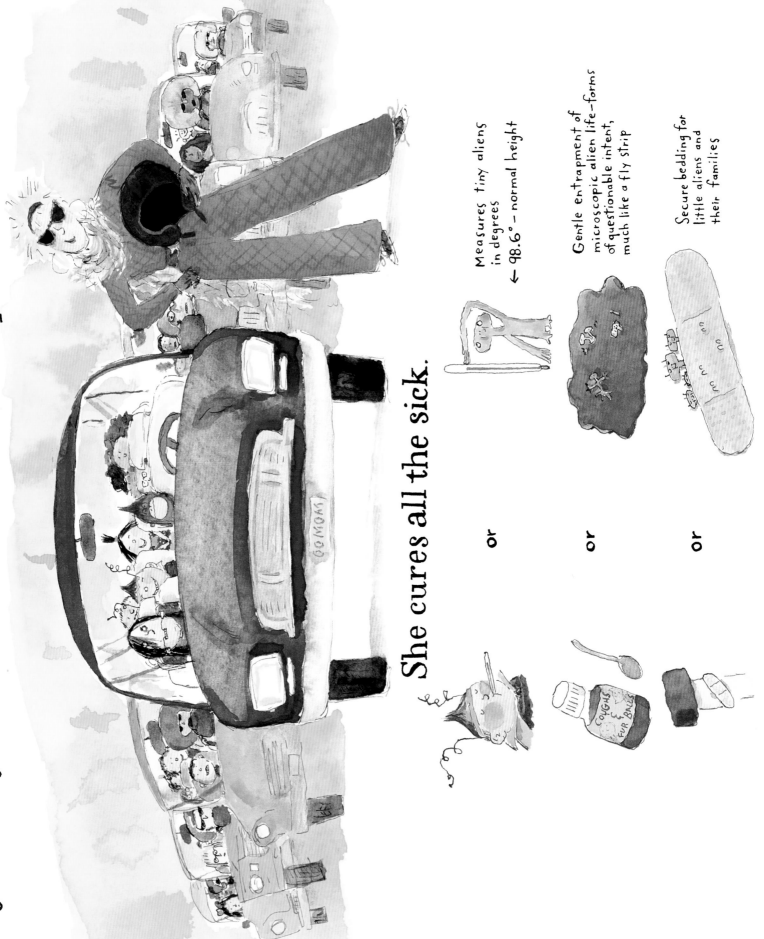

She cures all the sick.

Measures tiny aliens in degrees
← 98.6° – normal height

or

Gentle entrapment of microscopic alien life-forms of questionable intent, much like a fly strip

or

Secure bedding for little aliens and their families

or

She works every tool.

Important information
extractor

Top Secret
launchpad
for tiny
life-forms

Brain wave
Scrambler

Dangerous yet smooth landing strip

Ear probe for large
unidentifiable life-forms

Alien portion
control

Delicate mission tool

She ZOOMS in the car, and boy, it goes fast!

And those rocket ships,

guess *who* made them blast?

and backflips.

She makes my new kite
do spins

She flies all the planes.

She rows all the ships.

She molds every ball, carves rackets and bats.
And stealing the bases? She's way good at that!

She buzzed every every bee.
She spun every every spider.

She growled every bear.
She striped every tiger.

My mommy makes music, and boy, can she rock.

While we
hip and hop,

my mommy
moonwalks.

She rules the whole world
from her throne.
She's my queen.

My mommy is nice. She never is mean.

She pours all the seas
and sparkles each star.
And then she collects one
in my night-light jar.

And when she paints night
so jet black and deep,
my mother ship rocks me
gently to sleep.

I dream about how she gave me my start.
I love my mommy with all of my heart.

Then when I'm asleep all safe in my nest,
my mommy stays up and does all the rest.

My mommy hung the moon.
She tied it with string.

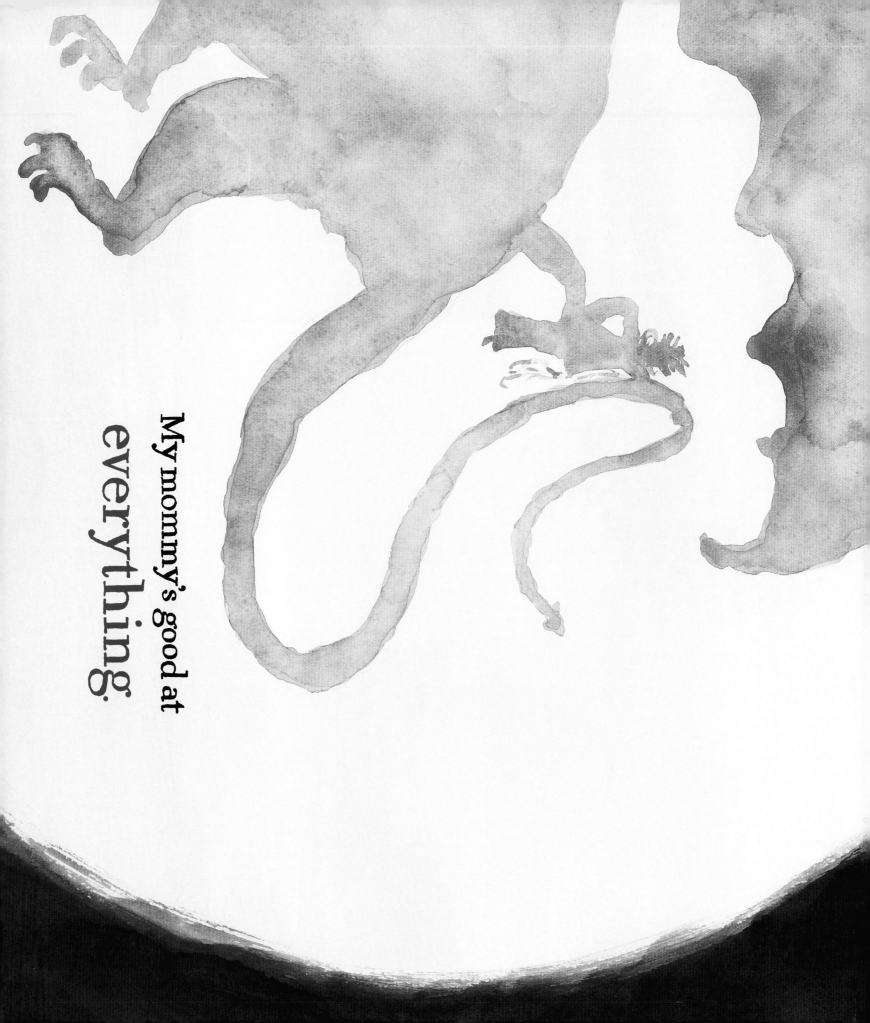

My mommy's good at
everything.

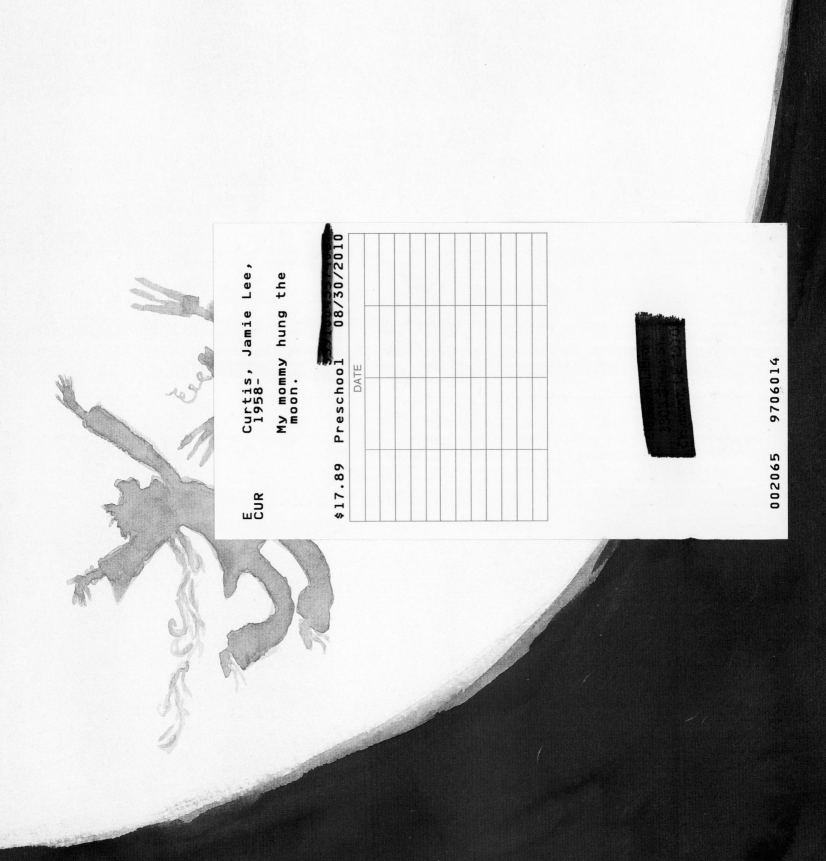